Dear Parents and Caregivers,

If your child is ready to learn how to read, then you've come to the right place! We want kids to reach for the stars as they begin their reading adventure. With Ready-to-Go!, this very first level has been carefully mapped out to launch their reading voyage.

All books in this level share the following:

★ Just the right length: each story has about 100 words, many of them repeated.

★ Sight words: frequently used words that children will come to recognize by sight, such as "the" and "can."

★ Word families: rhyming words used throughout the story for ease of recognition.

★ A guide at the beginning that prompts children to sound out the words before they start reading.

★ Questions at the end for children to re-engage with the story.

★ Fun stories starring children's favorite characters so learning to read is a blast.

These books will provide children with confidence in their reading abilities as they go from mastering the letters of the alphabet to understanding how those letters create words, sentences, and stories.

Blast off on this starry adventure . . . a universe of reading awaits!

Miffy's Adventures Big and Small

Miffy and the Band

Story written by May Nakamura
Based on the work of Dick Bruna

Ready-to-Read

Simon Spotlight
New York London Toronto Sydney New Delhi

Here is a list of all the words you will find in this book.
Sound them out before you begin reading the story.

Names:

Miffy

Dan

Melanie

Grunty

SIMON SPOTLIGHT
An imprint of Simon & Schuster Children's Publishing Division
1230 Avenue of the Americas, New York, New York 10020
This Simon Spotlight edition October 2018
Published in 2018 by Simon & Schuster, Inc. Publication licensed by Mercis Publishing bv, Amsterdam.
Stories and images are based on the work of Dick Bruna.
'Miffy and Friends' © copyright Mercis Media bv, all rights reserved.
All rights reserved, including the right of reproduction in whole or in part in any form.
SIMON SPOTLIGHT, READY-TO-READ, and colophon are registered trademarks of Simon & Schuster, Inc.
For information about special discounts for bulk purchases, please contact Simon & Schuster Special Sales at
1-866-506-1949 or business@simonandschuster.com.
Manufactured in the United States of America 0818 LAK
10 9 8 7 6 5 4 3 2 1
ISBN 978-1-5344-1624-6 (hc)
ISBN 978-1-5344-1623-9 (pbk)
ISBN 978-1-5344-1625-3 (eBook)

Word families:

"-ad"	→	glad	sad
"-ay"	→	day	play

Sight words:

all	and	are	can	is
the	this	to	try	what
will				

Bonus words:

band	cannot	guitar	help	recorder
tuba	violin			

Ready to go? Happy reading!

Don't miss the questions about the story
on the last page of this book.

This is Miffy.

This is the band.

The band
can play.

Melanie can play the guitar.

Dan can play
the violin.

Grunty can play
the tuba.

What can Miffy play?

Can Miffy play the recorder?

Miffy cannot
play the recorder.

The band
will try to help.

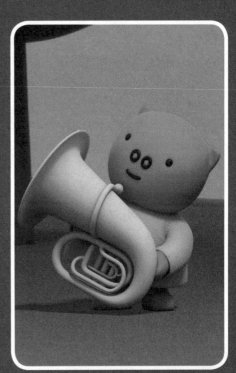

Can Miffy play the guitar?

Can Miffy play
the violin?

Can Miffy play the tuba?

Miffy cannot play.

Miffy is sad.

Miffy will try to play the recorder.

Miffy will try
and try.

Miffy will try all day.

Miffy can play
the recorder!

Miffy and the band are glad!

Now that you have read the story, can you answer these questions?

1. Who plays in the band?

2. What instruments do they play?

3. In this story, you read the words "day" and "play." Can you think of other words that rhyme with "day" and "play"?

Great job!
You are a reading star!